THE PROTÉGÉ

CASE FILES: POCKET-SIZED MURDER MYSTERIES

RACHEL AMPHLETT

SAXON PUBLISHING

The Protégé © 2025 by Rachel Amphlett

Originally published in *Thrill Rides: Sidekicks* © 2025

All rights reserved.

No part of this book may be reproduced in any form or by any electronic or mechanical means, including information storage and retrieval systems, without written permission from the author, except for the use of brief quotations in a book review.

This is a work of fiction. While the locations in this book are a mixture of real and imagined, the characters are totally fictitious. Any resemblance to actual people living or dead is entirely coincidental.

These pocket-sized murder mysteries are fast-paced quick reads and available in eBook, audiobook and print from Rachel's shop, major retailers and libraries.

Use the QR code for details about each short story and where to buy.

THE PROTÉGÉ

ONE

May 1936
  Near Wokingham, England

The road was a winding lane that had once been used by horse-drawn carriages until the motor car became popular.

A late spring was now turning to summer, and the bluebells had given way to rhododendrons bearing enormous blossoms of pink, mauve and red petals that were cradled amongst lush dark green leaves. Scots Pine trees towered above the rhododendrons, with silver birch, chestnut and rowan vying for space between the two. The ancient trees still bore the imprint of the original carriages, their boughs arching above the tarmac that was laid down over the old dirt and stone track ten years ago, their branches creating a green tunnel that horses had once trotted along.

The road undulated for the whole of its two miles and stretched between an unassuming crossroads and a main road that connected outlying villages to Reading.

Sunlight sparkled on wet leaves that glistened after a late-morning rain shower, and every few yards there was a house name displayed beside a gate built into a stone wall or wooden fence..

The six-bedroom house halfway along the road was, appropriately, called 'Treetops', for it rested in the arc of a crescent-shaped lawn framed by pine trees and shrubs. Beyond its gate was a gravel driveway that had been freshly combed that morning, and a landscaped garden with flowering borders that had been trimmed just so.

It had a slate tile roof, red brick chimneys at each end, and ivy covering rendered walls that had been tastefully plastered to leave the original dark oak beams exposed.

Bernard Hackley-Wilson and his wife of almost thirty years, Isobel, were in the sitting room at half-past one when the muffled sound of the doorbell reverberated along the hallway.

Neither moved.

Bernard shuffled in his wing-backed leather armchair, flapped the pages of his broadsheet Sunday newspaper and blinked while his eyes adjusted to the small text of an article in the bottom right-hand corner. Isobel wiggled her socked toes before curling her legs up onto the two-seater settee that had been delivered last week from a boutique in London and took a sip from a glass of gin.

Three ice cubes clinked against the crystal, and a moment later Bernard heard familiar footsteps walk from the direction of the scullery, pass the closed sitting room door and stop at the far end of the hallway.

He lowered his newspaper, cocked his head and

strained his ears at the sound of the door opening, and then the sound of murmured voices reached him.

"Are you expecting anyone, my love?" he asked.

Isobel shook her head, then lowered her glass. "Not today." Her voice was slow, considered. "Marjorie sent a message to say she won't be back from Paris until Wednesday."

Bernard looked down at the newspaper, frowned as he read the headline for the story that had captured his attention, then folded the broadsheet and put it on the armrest. That done, he clasped his hands in his lap.

And waited.

———

The butler, John, had been with the family since he was fourteen.

He had worked in the stables before being transferred to the kitchen at the age of seventeen after his father had died in the Great War and his mother moved to an estate near Brockenhurst to work as a scullery maid.

It had been Isobel who had spotted the young man's potential during a garden party five summers ago when John's predecessor, an elderly man in his late sixties, passed away while carrying a silver tray laden with champagne flutes. His body was only discovered in the icehouse after guests complained about the lack of available refreshments.

Isobel had been distraught.

A replacement had to be found, of course, and noticing how John had emerged from the kitchens with a fresh tray of drinks hastily dressed in one of the old butler's suits while he calmly assuring her guests that the champagne was of the correct vintage, Isobel went to find her husband.

Upon settling the previous incumbent's funeral expenses on behalf of his family, she insisted that Bernard send them a stipend each year at Christmas. That done, John was promoted to be the family's full-time butler and had since proven he was a trustworthy and dependable member of the household ever since.

He rapped his knuckles twice against the oak door, two precisely executed knocks that exuded confidence with a measure of respect.

The door remained shut until Bernard cleared his throat and called. "Come."

John stepped inside and moved swiftly to the right to make way for their mysterious guest. "Detective Inspector George McKlinnon, sir."

Bernard frowned as a man in his mid-forties entered the room.

The detective was dressed in a smart grey suit with a navy tie. His moustache was tidy and waxed and his brown hair was worn a little longer than current societal expectations without being outrageous. He held a black fedora in his left hand, which he tapped against his leg. His black leather shoes were shone to the standards expected within military circles and his blue eyes were keen as he looked first at Bernard, then Isobel.

His gaze moved back to Bernard before he spoke. "I'm sorry to interrupt your afternoon, sir, but I must speak to you about an urgent matter that has arisen."

Bernard's attention flickered to John. "That will be all."

"Sir."

The door closed behind the butler, and a silence followed his exit until Isobel cleared her throat.

"What sort of urgent matter, inspector?"

"A most troubling one." McKlinnon moved across the room until he was standing beside the settee opposite Bernard's chair. He didn't sit. "Last night, a young man in his twenties was found stabbed only a mile away from here, just along from Mr and Mrs Brecketts' house."

"Oh, my goodness," Isobel murmured. The ice cubes clinked against the crystal glass as she lowered her feet to the rug and sat upright. "Is he all right?"

"I'm afraid not, madam. I'm sorry to say that he passed away not long after midnight despite being taken to the hospital in Reading. The doctor informs me that it appears that the young man was stabbed in the abdomen and left to die at the side of the road."

Isobel looked over her shoulder at the sound of footsteps passing the sash window behind the settee, her mouth opening in a little 'o' of shock as a uniformed policeman walked past, his gaze firmly on the ground. "Who's that?"

"One of my men, police constable Harry Swinson," McKlinnon explained. "I have him checking the perimeter of your property for any sign of trespass that might explain how the victim's killer escaped notice."

Bernard felt a chill cross his shoulders. "Are we safe? Are you telling us that there's a madman roaming the area?"

"I think it prudent to make sure all your doors are locked in the evening," said McKlinnon, "but I'd like to ask you both some questions, if I may?"

"Of course." Bernard waved his hand at the man and settled into his armchair and watched while the inspector withdrew a black leather-bound notebook and a pencil from his jacket pocket. "Proceed."

———

McKlinnon flicked to a new page and wrote something at the top of it.

Bernard listened to the scratch of the pencil across the cheap paper, the ticking from a gilt-framed carriage clock on the marble mantlepiece keeping a steady beat while, beyond the sash window, a robin chirruped from the ivy winding its way around the granite stonework that framed the glass panes.

Eventually, the inspector looked up from his notebook. "First of all, may I ask where you were last night, sir?"

"I had business at the Courtneys' estate in Winnersh until eight o'clock, and then I came back here for a late supper with my wife."

"And from which direction did you travel home, sir?"

"The usual, via Barkham."

"Which would have taken you directly past the Brecketts' house, is that correct?"

"Yes, yes it would." Bernard paused, and frowned. "Why?"

"It's hard to tell how long he had lain there, because the young man wasn't found until almost ten o'clock, but did you see anything unusual on your way home?"

"I didn't, no. The lightning is rather dim along that stretch of road."

"It is, you're right sir." McKlinnon paused in his note-taking for a moment, contemplating the rug beneath the coffee table. Then his gaze snapped back to Bernard. "Let me rephrase that. Did you see anyone walking along the road, or anyone acting suspiciously at the side of the road as you drove by?"

Bernard thought for a moment. He remembered leaving the Courtneys' house, getting into the car and winding down the window to wave cheerio to Walter, who had remained on the doorstep with a glass of port in his hand. After that, the drive home had been a blur. It was so familiar to him that the scenery had passed by without a second glance.

"No," he said eventually. "I didn't notice anything at all, I'm afraid."

The inspector turned to Isobel. "Mrs Hackley-Wilson, I wonder if you might have seen anything?"

"Oh, I was here all last night," she said. "A friend of mine was due to telephone from Paris, and I had to wait for her call."

"Can you confirm what time your husband arrived home?"

"No later than twenty minutes past eight." Isobel gave a shy smile, then raised the tumbler to her lips and drained the last of the gin and tonic. She peered at the empty glass as if wondering where all the contents had gone. "I remember that, because I heard the car's wheels on the gravel and looked at the clock. It gave me just enough time to tell Alice to prepare supper."

"Alice?"

"Our cook and cleaner."

"Thank you." McKlinnon snapped shut his notebook and put it away.

"Will that be all, inspector?" Bernard asked.

"As you can appreciate, with the rain this morning it's proving very difficult to recover any evidence, so these house-to-house enquiries are necessary to our investigation. I apologise for the interruption."

"Not at all," said Isobel. "How wretched for that poor man's family. If there's anything else we can do..."

"Yes, I'd like to speak to your staff please."

"The staff?" Bernard frowned. "Why on earth would you want to do that?"

"It's simply procedure," said the inspector. "To see if they might have observed something that will help with our enquiries."

"I believe they were all here last night," said Isobel. "I can certainly vouch for Alice, and for John—our butler."

"Is there anyone else working here?"

"Our gardener, Edward, lives in a cottage in the village," Bernard explained. "He only comes here on Tuesdays and Thursdays, so he'll be of no use to you. William, our gamekeeper, had his appendix out last week and won't be back to work until next month."

"All the same," McKlinnon said. "I'd like to speak with Alice and John, please."

Bernard reached out for a woven cord that dangled from the wall beside his chair. "I'll summon them for you."

"Not to worry, sir. I'll go and find them myself. Thank you for your time."

———

John, the butler, was polishing a candlestick with a stained blue cloth when McKlinnon found him in the kitchen.

The man had taken up one end of a long wooden bench for the task and wore protective gloves to guard against the pugnacious chemicals that he was rubbing into the silverware. A stained apron covered his uniform, although he had removed his jacket which now hung over the back of one of the upright wooden chairs tucked under the bench.

He stopped rubbing the candlestick at the sight of the detective inspector, the cloth held at mid-sweep. "Help you?"

"Possibly," said McKlinnon, removing his notebook. "Could you confirm your full name please?"

"Why?"

"Just answer the question please."

"John Marlow."

"Address?"

"Here."

"All the time?"

John tossed the cloth onto the bench but set down the now-gleaming candelabra with a little more reverence. "All the time."

"Where were you last night, between the hours of six and ten o'clock?"

"Here, working."

"Can anyone vouch for you?"

"Mrs Hackley-Wilson. She asked me to make sure that Alice used the parsley growing next to the stable block in today's lunch and then rang for me at eight o'clock for some fresh tea."

"Tea?"

"That's right, yes."

"At eight o'clock at night?"

"Yes."

"Have you seen strangers around the house in the past twenty-four hours?"

"No." John cocked his head. "What's going on, if you don't mind my asking?"

"A young man was stabbed just along the road from the Brecketts' house last night," said McKlinnon, more than aware of the weariness in his voice as he closed his notebook once more. "Therefore, we're interviewing residents in the neighbourhood as part of our enquiries."

John blew out his cheeks before picking up the cloth. "Terrible news. I hope you catch the bastard who did that to him."

"As do I, Mr Marlow."

———

McKlinnon found Alice outside the kitchen door, plucking at a thick rosemary shrub that filled the afternoon air with a sweet aroma.

She was wearing a typical uniform comprising a black dress and white mop hat to keep her hair out of the way. There was a egg-coloured stain on the dress that had evidently escaped the protection of an apron while cooking, but her stout black shoes were shined to perfection.

She looked over her shoulder at the sound of his approach, her ruddy cheeks and crow's feet accentuating a face that was open and friendly. "Help you?"

"Detective Inspector George McKlinnon, Miss…?"

"Wendrow. Alice Wendrow." She straightened, her knuckles rubbing the base of her spine while she twirled the springs of rosemary between the fingers of her left hand. "What's the police doing here, then? I saw your youngster wandering around."

"I'm investigating the death of a man not much older than him," said the inspector. "He was killed along the road there, close to the Brecketts' house yesterday evening."

Alice paled, the back rubbing stopped, and her expression turned to one of horror. "Killed?"

"Stabbed, we believe. My men and I are currently searching for evidence and any information about the incident, which is why I'd like to ask you some questions."

"Questions?"

"Yes. Will here do, or…?"

Alice glanced over his shoulder, then shook her head. "Out here. No need to bother the family, is there?"

"I've already interviewed Mr and Mrs Hackley-Wilson."

"Oh. All right then, go on."

"Where were you last night between the hours of six and ten o'clock?"

"Here, working. John came back to the kitchen with a message from the missus at five o'clock reminding me about today's lunch, and then again at eight to fetch a pot of tea for her. I then prepared supper when Mr Hackley-Wilson returned from visiting friends."

"I thought Mrs H-W was more of a gin drinker."

"Gin?" Alice gave a nervous chuckle. "Oh no, sir. Maybe a tipple now and again, and champagne at parties, but she's not a big drinker."

McKlinnon paused, updated his notes, and looked past the cook to where the herb garden gave way to fruit trees bearing pink and white blossom. Beyond those there was an immaculate lawn bordered by alder and birch trees that shielded the property from being seen from the road. "Have you noticed anything peculiar over the past two days perhaps?"

"No, not that I can remember. It's always very quiet around here,," said Alice with a shiver. "Which is why your news about that poor lad is so horrible. I can't imagine who would do something like that to someone."

McKlinnon sighed, and gestured to the paved path that wound through the garden. "I presume that will take me back to the driveway?"

"It will, sir."

"Then, thank you for your time Miss Wendrow."

———

Isobel stood at the front window of the reception room and watched the detective inspector walking back towards his car, then wandered to the settee, slid the crystal tumbler across the coffee table and sank against the settee cushions.

The tumbler left a watery streak across the mahogany surface that would surely cause Alice no end of trouble to remove, but that was a problem for her, not Isobel.

Right now, her vision was blurring, and she held a

hand to her lips as a small hiccup escaped. "Ugh. I always hated that stuff."

"Then, why drink it?" Bernard asked, his brow furrowing.

She shot her husband a pointed look, then reached across to select a magazine from the pile she had been saving that week and flicked to a page showing the latest society photographs from London and further afield. Sighing, she blinked to offset the swirling text underneath the images. "Because I had to, darling."

Bernard picked up his newspaper once more, flapped it open to the financial pages, and scratched absently at his chin. "Strange woman."

George McKlinnon stalked towards his Morris Eight and contemplated the notebook that weighed heavy in his jacket pocket.

He and his men had spent most of the night and all morning working, first at the crime scene and now scouring the surrounding countryside for clues – and a killer. On top of that, he had a new officer to train in the ways of Berkshire Constabulary and a chief inspector expecting results before the local media caught wind of the investigation.

Reaching the automobile, he removed his keys from his pocket then looked over the roof of the car at the sound of rapid footsteps walking across the gravel.

Harry Swinson, the new lad, was hurrying towards him from the direction of a converted stable block that looked as if it was now used to house

Bernard Hackley-Wilson's collection of sports cars, given the gleaming metalwork that caught the light from the open wooden doors. There was a second stable block on the opposite side of the house, outside of which was a heap of dirty straw and four fresh hay bales, so evidently the family's horses were still used from time to time.

Harry bore an expression of anticipation, and as George walked around the car to meet him, he noticed the young officer was holding a package wrapped in paper.

"What have you been up to, Swinson?" he began. "I thought I told you to make a thorough inspection of the house and garden while I was conducting interviews?"

"I did that, sir." Harry's voice was breathless. "But I thought I'd look in the stables in case our culprit was hiding there."

George conceded the point with a nod. "Fair enough. Was he?"

"No, sir. But I did find this." Harry thrust the parcel at him. "I found a pile of old newspapers next to the scullery door and wrapped it to keep it safe after I unbolted it."

Intrigued, George took it from him. It was heavy, and whatever was inside was of an uneven size, long at one end with a forked shape at the other. Cradling it in his hand while he carefully unwrapped the newspaper from it, he blinked when he saw the chrome plating.

He glanced up at Harry. "A hood ornament?"

"Look closer, sir. There's blood on it."

George pulled the last of the newspaper away, revealing the brass mascot in all its glory, and then saw the dark stains covering the forked design. "Well, I'll be damned."

"Our victim wasn't stabbed, sir," said Harry. "He was hit by the car, wasn't he?"

"And Mrs Hackley-Wilson isn't a gin drinker," George concluded. "She's covering up for her husband who was driving after drinking too much at dinner last night."

He re-wrapped the hood ornament and handed it to Harry.

"You'll go far, young Swinson," he said, slapping his protégé across the shoulders. "Now, let's go and see what Mr Bernard Hackley-Wilson has to say for himself, shall we?"

THE END

ABOUT THE AUTHOR

Rachel Amphlett is a USA Today bestselling author of crime fiction and spy thrillers, many of which have been translated worldwide.

Her novels are available in eBook, print, and audiobook formats from libraries and retailers as well as her website shop.

A keen traveller, Rachel has both Australian and British citizenship.

Find out more about Rachel's books at: www.rachelamphlett.com.